ABC DANNY

by
Mia Coulton

MaryRuth Books Inc
Cleveland

ABC Danny

Published by:
MaryRuth Books, Inc.
18660 Ravenna Road
Building 2
Chagrin Falls, OH 44023
877.834.1105
www.maryruthbooks.com

10 9 8 7 6 5 4 3

Library of Congress Control Number: 2008911611

ISBN 978-1-933624-34-1

SPC/0211/21254

To my little peppercorn

A a

apple

B b

bee

Cc

cat

D d

dog

E e

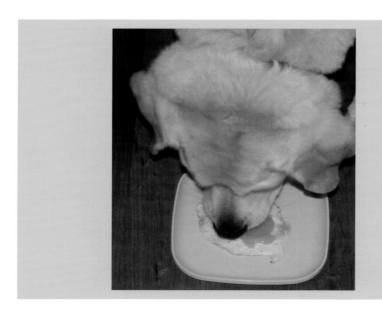

egg

F f

fish

G g

girl

H h

hat

I i

igloo

J j

jelly beans

K k

king

L l

leaves

M m

mask

N n

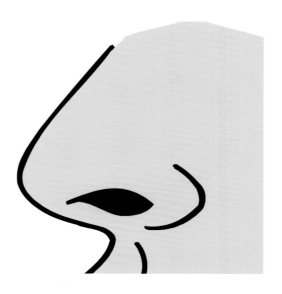

nose

O o

octopus

P p

pumpkins

Q q

quilt

R r

raccoon

S s

socks

Tt

towel

U u

umbrella

V v

vacuum

W w

wagon

X x

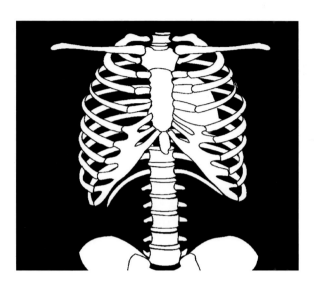

x-ray

Y y

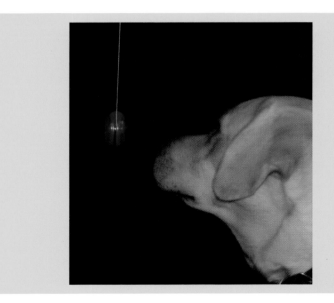

yo-yo

Z z

zipper

a b c d e f g
h i j k l m n o p
q r s t u and v
w x y and z

Now I know my ABCs
Next time won't you sing with me?

THE

END